KU-668-596

For Ring.
M.C.

DEAN

First published in Great Britain 2020 by Farshore
This edition published 2023 by Dean, part of Farshore
An imprint of HarperCollins*Publishers*
1 London Bridge Street, London SE1 9GF
www.farshore.co.uk

HarperCollins*Publishers*
Macken House, 39/40 Mayor Street Upper,
Dublin 1, D01 C9W8, Ireland

Text and Illustrations © Matt Carr 2020
Matt Carr has asserted his moral rights.

ISBN 978 0 0086 1710 3
Printed in China
001

A CIP catalogue record for this title is available from the British Library.

MIX
Paper | Supporting
responsible forestry
FSC™ C007454

This book is produced from independently certified FSC™ paper
to ensure responsible forest management.

For more information visit: www.harpercollins.co.uk/green

RHINOCORN RULES!

Matt Carr

DEAN

Ron looked the same as any other rhinoceros.
He was big, he was grey and he had
a pointy thing on the top of his nose.

But Ron *felt* different.

Now, Ron knew the THREE RHINO RULES...

Rule 1: Be alone.

Rule 2: Be a bit grumpy.

What are you looking at?

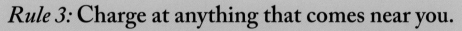

Rule 3: Charge at anything that comes near you.

Get out of my way!

He loved FUN,
ART, LAUGHTER and MUSIC!
He was just bursting
with IDEAS and JOY!

Ron wanted to share this with everyone, but because he was a rhino, none of the other animals would go near him.

It's a rhino! Run!

And when he did meet up with another rhino,
they didn't want to chat . . .

they just wanted to CHARGE!

Life wasn't much fun
for poor Ron . . .

until one hot afternoon at the watering hole, when he looked at his grey reflection in the water.

"If only I could show everyone my **TRUE COLOURS**," he thought. "Then I'd be sure to make friends."

This gave Ron a great idea!

First, he rolled around in the dust until he was completely covered in it.

Next, he gathered berries and leaves and smooshed them up to make different colours.

SPLAT!

And then he got

CREATIVE!

It was very messy, but it was

GREAT FUN!

The sticky colours soon dried in the hot sun.
Ron was a walking **WORK OF ART!**

He felt

A-MA-ZING!

The meerkats were the first
to notice Ron. Instead of running
away, they all gathered around him.
They were very impressed
by this colourful new animal.

"ARE YOU A UNICORN?"

asked one of
the meerkat pups.

Ron thought about it for a moment.

"ER, NO...I'M A RHINOCORN!"

The other animals were very excited to meet Ron.

He made lots of new friends . . .

and had lots of FUN!

For the first time in his life . . .

Nice throw!

Ron was HAPPY!

But word of **RON THE RHINOCORN** soon spread . . .

and the other rhinos weren't at all happy!

Ron felt terribly sad.
All he wanted was to make
friends and have fun.

Now he just felt
silly for breaking
the rhino rules.

But Ron's new meerkat pals
were having none of it!

"As long as you're happy with who
you are, that's all that counts!"

The brave little meerkats stood up
for Ron and made a very good point.

"Look at you, all together,
and all getting on with each other,"
they laughed. "Looks like you've
ALL BROKEN THE RHINO RULES!"

It slowly dawned on the other rhinos
that they *had* broken their own rules.

One by one they started to laugh.

"You're right," they agreed.
"We have enjoyed hanging out together!"

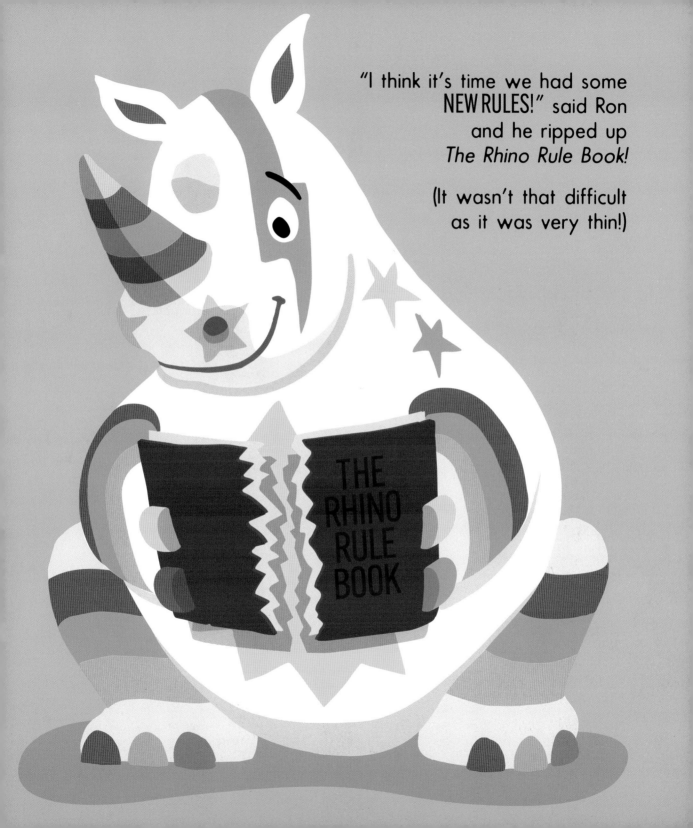

"I think it's time we had some **NEW RULES!**" said Ron and he ripped up *The Rhino Rule Book!*

(It wasn't that difficult as it was very thin!)

And so Ron created three much-better rules
for everyone to follow . . .

Rule 1: **Be yourself.**

Rule 2: **Make lots
of friends.**

MEERKAT CREATIVE
Paint Service
NO JOB TOO BIG!

DID YOU RHI-KNOW?

Even though rhinos are huge they are **HERBIVORES** and only feed on plants.

Rhinos don't get together much but when they do it's called a **CRASH!**

White rhinos are actually grey! They weigh the same as **30 PEOPLE!**

Male rhinos mark out their territory with **POO!**

There are **5** different kinds of rhino: white, black, Sumatran, Javan and Indian.

The word **RHINOCEROS** means 'NOSE HORN'.

Rhino horns are made out of the same stuff as your fingernails!

Sadly, rhinos are one of the most endangered species on Earth. The main threat to these amazing animals is illegal hunting.